The LOST (AND FOUND) Balloon

By Celeste Jenkins

Illustrated by Maria Bogade

Aladdin

NEW YORK   LONDON   TORONTO   SYDNEY   NEW DELHI

For Madeline and Ella —C.J.

To my family—

I wouldn't be who I am without all of you. —M.B.

ALADDIN An imprint of Simon & Schuster Children's Publishing Division 1230 Avenue of the Americas, New York, NY 10020 Text copyright © 2012 by Celeste Jenkins

Illustrations copyright © 2012 by Maria Bogade All rights reserved, including the right of reproduction in whole or in part in any form. ALADDIN is a trademark of Simon & Schuster,

Inc., and related logo is a registered trademark of Simon & Schuster, Inc. For information about special discounts for bulk purchases, please contact Simon & Schuster Special Sales at

1-866-506-1949 or business@simonandschuster.com. The Simon & Schuster Speakers Bureau can bring authors to your live event. For more information or to book an event contact

the Simon & Schuster Speakers Bureau at 1-866-248-3049 or visit our website at www.simonspeakers.com. Designed by Karin Paprocki The text of this book was set in Alghera Regular.

Manufactured in the China 0313 SCP 2 4 6 8 10 9 7 5 3 1 This book has been cataloged by the Library of Congress. ISBN 978-1-4424-6697-5 ISBN 978-1-4424-6699-9 (eBook)

Molly O'Doon
had a balloon
red and shiny and round.

With a blue and white string,
a silly tail-of-a-thing,
that hung long and straight to the ground.

Molly tied on a note
and set it afloat
with hopes it soon would be found.

Up to the sky.

High, high, high, high.

Balloon sailing.
String trailing.

Above leafy trees.
Over flowers and bees.

Close to a cloud.
Sounds not so loud.

Barking dogs hushed.
Honking cars shushed.

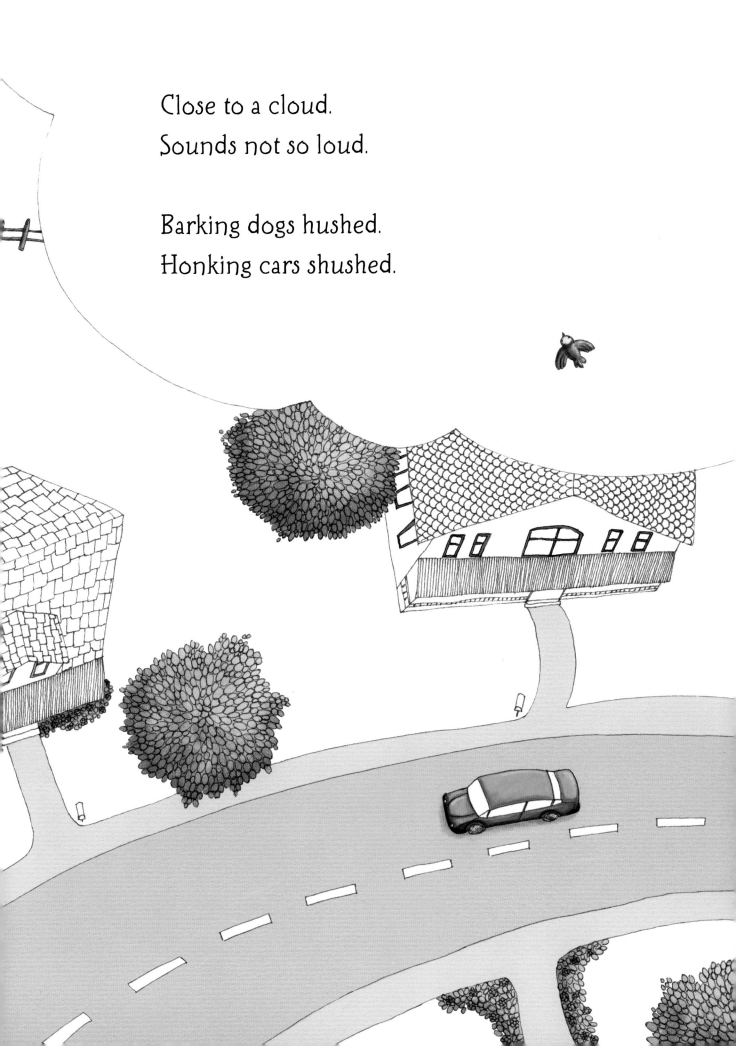

Each shrinking house
small like a mouse.

Fields into rugs.
Cows into bugs.

Sun sinking low.
Gold colors glow.

Sun goes down.
Dark all around.

Twinkling lights under a glittery wonder.

Silhouette on the moon
of a proud balloon.

Wind blows.
Balloon goes.

Here comes the sun.
Night now is done.

Balloon sinks lower.
Sails a bit slower.

Patchwork below
seems to grow.

Dots into ducks.
Ants into trucks.

Town getting nearer.
Sounds getting clearer.

Blue bird sings.
Tower bell rings.

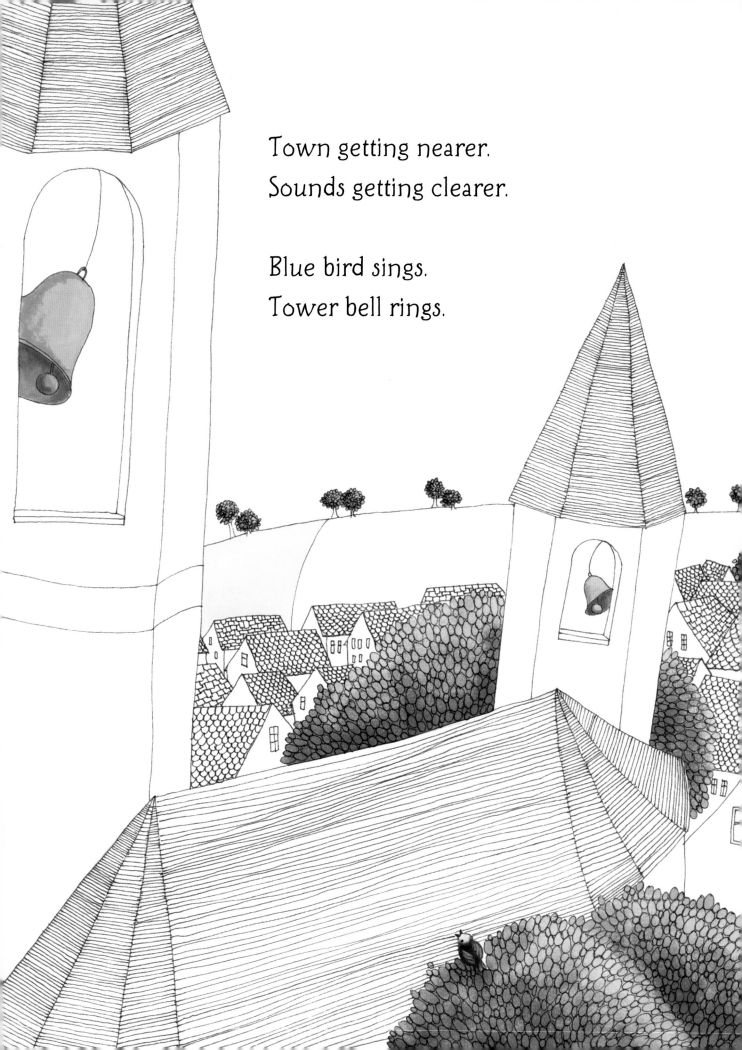

Balloon red and round
heads for the ground.

Slowly deflating.
Yard below waiting.

Sandbox.
Shoes and socks.

Sun hat.
Orange cat.

Katie McCloat
sat down, read the note.

What's your town like?

Do you have a bike?

Tell me about where you are.

Do you ever play ball?

Is your house big or small?

Do you ride in a spaceship or car?

Please write back today.

904 Clover Way

Madison, Wisconsin, USA

(Earth)

The address that she read
"Is like mine!" Katie said.
But instead of a six was a four.

Katie did not run far—
past her mailbox and car,
and knocked on the house right next door!

Molly O'Doon
saw the balloon,
smiled and said, "Let's play."

Katie grinned too.

"Nice to meet you.

My family moved here yesterday!"